The Mayflower Compact

The Mayflower Compact

Dennis Brindell Fradin

 **Marshall Cavendish** Benchmark

New York

Acknowledgment

With special thanks to James W. Baker, Curator, Alden House Historic Site,
for reviewing the text of this book.

Marshall Cavendish Benchmark
99 White Plains Road
Tarrytown, NY 10591
www.marshallcavendish.us

Text and map copyright © 2007 by Marshall Cavendish Corporation
Map on p. 17 by XNR Productions

All Internet sites were available and accurate when sent to press.

Library of Congress Cataloging-in-Publication Data

Fradin, Dennis B.
The Mayflower Compact / by Dennis Brindell Fradin.
p. cm. — (Turning points of United States history)
Includes bibliographical references and index.
ISBN-13: 978-0-7614-2125-2
ISBN-10: 0-7614-2125-4
1. Mayflower Compact (1620)—Juvenile literature. 2. Pilgrims (New
Plymouth Colony)—Juvenile literature. 3. Mayflower (Ship)—Juvenile
literature. 4. Massachusetts—History—New Plymouth, 1620-1691—Juvenile
literature. I. Title II. Series: Fradin, Dennis B. Turning points of
United States history.
F68.F78 2006
974.4'02—dc22
2005016021

Photo Research by Connie Gardner

Title page: Oil and tempera painting of the signing of the Mayflower Compact, by N. C. Wyeth, 1940.

Cover Photo: The Granger Collection
Title Page: The Granger Collection
The photographs in the book are used by permission and through the courtesy of: *Corbis*: Burstein Collection, 6, 9, 40-41; Bettmann, 20, 23, 29, 32;
Getty Images: Hulton Archive, 10, 16, 18, 30; *The Granger Collection*: 11, 24, 28; *NorthWind Picture Archives*: 12, 26, 34, 35, 36; *Art Resource*: New York
Public Library, 14; *Brown Brothers*: 22.

Editorial Director: Michelle Bisson
Art Director: Anahid Hamparian
Printed in China
1 3 5 6 4 2

Contents

The Mayflower in Plymouth Harbor, painted by William Halsall, around 1900.

CHAPTER ONE

"They Were Strangers and Pilgrims on the Earth"

On a late summer's day nearly four **centuries** ago, a ship called the *Mayflower* set sail from Plymouth, England. The date was September 6, 1620, by the calendar then in use. Aboard the vessel were 102 passengers who would become known as the Pilgrims, plus a crew of about 30 men. They were bound for America, 3,000 miles away.

The story of the Pilgrims began long before the *Mayflower* put out to sea. In the early 1600s, England did not offer freedom of religion. James I, who became king in 1603, expected everyone to follow one religion, the Church of England. Men and women who did not belong to this church, or who criticized it, could be punished.

The Old Calendar and the New

Over the centuries, the calendar has undergone major changes. What was September 6, 1620 to the Pilgrims is September 16, 1620, according to our modern calendar. To convert the old calendar dates to modern ones, just add ten days. For example, the Pilgrims signed the Mayflower Compact on November 11, 1620, by their calendar, which would be November 21, 1620, by ours. The dates in this book are those the Pilgrims used, which we call Old Style. Our modern calendar dates are known as New Style.

Nonetheless, many people felt that the Church of England had become too involved with **rituals** and politics. Some of them broke away from the Church of England and held their own simple services, which instead focused on the Bible. These people, called **Separatists**, tried to keep their worship secret by meeting in private homes and barns.

William Brewster was a leader of a Separatist group that met in Scrooby, a village in central England. The Scrooby Separatists caught the attention of English officials in 1607. They lost their jobs, and some were jailed. In 1608 most of the Scrooby Separatists fled to the Netherlands, which offered more religious freedom than any other nation in Europe. By 1609 they had settled in Leiden, a city where they lived for eleven years. The Separatists

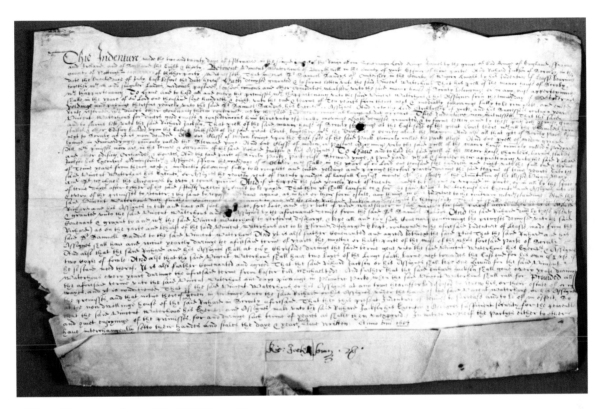

The Charter, signed by William Brewster.

from Scrooby worshipped in peace in Leiden, and were joined there by other English Separatists.

But as time passed, the Separatists found that life in the Netherlands had drawbacks. Earning a living was a challenge. Besides, the adults still viewed themselves as English. They were upset that their children, growing up in the Netherlands, were **abandoning** English ways.

Where might they go and be able to worship in peace, earn a living, and maintain English customs? At this time England had only one **permanent**

A Separatist is burnt at the stake to the delight of followers of the Church of England. This woodcut is from an 1855 version of John Milton's *The Pilgrim's Progress*.

American **colony**. It was what we call the Virginia Colony, which had been started in 1607 with the founding of Jamestown. The Separatists decided to create their own American colony. They knew it would be very difficult. Hunger, disease, and other hardships had killed most of the English people who had settled Virginia in its first several years. But the Separatists were determined to have a place of their own.

This engraving shows Pilgrims leaving the Flemish coast for America, where they hoped to be able to practice their religion without fear.

They returned to England, where they prepared for their voyage. King James I was glad to get rid of the Separatists, who were expected to settle at the site of what is now New York City. In England the Separatists were joined by some non-Separatists who also wanted to move to America.

Twice in the summer of 1620, the voyagers set out in two ships, the *Mayflower*, and a smaller vessel called the *Speedwell*. Both times, the two ships had to return to England because the *Speedwell* was "leakie as a seive," as a

The departure of the Pilgrims on the *Speedwell* from Delfthaven, The Netherlands.

traveler reported. Finally the *Speedwell* was abandoned as unseaworthy. The 102 men, women, and children who were sailing to America crowded onto the *Mayflower*. On that late summer day in 1620 they headed out to sea.

Actually, only about forty of the *Mayflower's* passengers were Separatists. The rest were English people hoping to make their fortunes or begin a new life in the New World. But the entire group later became known as the **Pilgrims**. This was probably because William Bradford, a Separatist leader, wrote that the travelers "knew they were pilgrims" when they embarked on their dangerous journey. He took the word "**pilgrims**" from chapter 11 of the New Testament book Epistle to the Hebrews, in which it says:

They were strangers and pilgrims on the earth . . . .
But now they desire a better country.

The *Mayflower* at sea, shown in a painting from 1876.

CHAPTER TWO

The Trip Across the Ocean

Compared to today's oceangoing vessels, the *Mayflower* was tiny. It was just ninety feet (twenty-seven meters) long—the distance from home plate to first base in major league baseball. On board were at least two dogs that the Pilgrims were taking with them to the New World. There were probably also some cats aboard, whose job it was to keep the *Mayflower* free of rats.

The travelers suffered almost constant discomfort. There were no toilets, so they used buckets. There was so little room that some of the Pilgrims slept in the shallop, a boat stored below decks. Meals consisted of biscuits, salted pork and beef, and boiled beans and peas. The voyagers had no opportunity to wash their clothing during the entire two-month voyage.

What's in a Name?

The Pilgrims liked unusual names. Aboard the *Mayflower* were boys named Love Brewster, Wrestling Brewster, and Resolved White, and girls named Humility Cooper and Remember Allerton. As the *Mayflower* lay off Cape Cod, a son was born to Susanna and William White. Since the Pilgrims were looking for a place to settle, his parents named the baby Peregrine, a Latin name meaning "Wanderer." Peregrine White, the first English child to be born in what is now Massachusetts, lived to the age of eighty-three.

To make matters worse, the weather was sometimes stormy during the ocean crossing. As the *Mayflower* was tossed about by the howling winds and rolling ocean, many Pilgrims became seasick. During a storm, twenty-eight-year-old John Howland fell overboard. He was sinking into the deep when he managed to grab a ship's line and was pulled back aboard.

The Mayflower Compact was signed by the male Pilgrims who crossed the Atlantic in 1620. Among the signers were William Brewster, William Bradford, and Miles Standish.

One Pilgrim, a servant named William Butten, as well as one of the sailors, died during the voyage. One baby was born. Since the infant entered the world at sea, his parents, Elizabeth and Stephen Hopkins, named him Oceanus.

The morning of November 9, 1620, brought a beautiful sight: land! They were approaching Cape Cod, a long **peninsula** shaped like a fishing hook that today is part of Massachusetts. The Pilgrims were well north

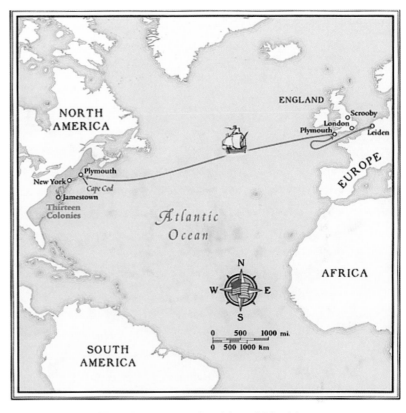

The Route to the New World

of where they had intended to settle, so the captain turned the *Mayflower* toward what is now New York. But the vessel, fighting rough weather, was in danger of being wrecked along the cape. The Pilgrims held a meeting and decided to stay in what is now Massachusetts. The *Mayflower* anchored at Cape Cod's Provincetown Harbor. There, the Pilgrims fell to their knees on the ship's deck and thanked God for landing them safely after more than sixty days at sea.

William Bradford (1755–1795), the only traveler on the *Mayflower* with a university education, is thought to have been the author of the Mayflower Compact.

CHAPTER THREE

The Mayflower Compact

Meanwhile, trouble was brewing on the *Mayflower*. Some non-Separatists were starting to **mutiny**, William Bradford reported. They threatened that, once ashore, they wouldn't settle with the Separatists but would go off on their own.

To succeed, the Separatists realized, their colony would need everyone to stay together and cooperate. They also knew why the non-Separatists were rebelling. They were afraid that, once on land, they would have little say about running things while the Separatists would control everything. By November 11, Separatist leaders had produced a paper guaranteeing certain rights to all the adult males who had sailed to America on the *Mayflower*. (In those days, women were generally excluded from politics and legal matters.)

A Poem about a Pact

In his famous poem *Western Star*, Stephen Vincent Benét wrote some wonderful lines about the Mayflower Compact:

[The] leaders thought it well
To draw a compact, binding their own together
In a lawful government for the town to be.
—And that was to be a cornerstone, in time,
Of something they never visioned from first to last . . . .
—And the seed is sown, and it grows in the deep earth,
And from it comes what the sower never dreamed.

The signing of the Mayflower Compact, as shown in a painting by E. Moran that hangs in Pilgrim Hall, Plymouth, Massachusetts.

William Brewster, the only Pilgrim with a university education, may have been the main author of this **document**, which was written aboard the ship. William Bradford and John Carver may have helped Brewster.

Since it was created aboard the *Mayflower*, the agreement became known as the **Mayflower Compact**. It contained just two hundred words. To understand the Mayflower Compact, it helps to know a few things. *Ye* is an old way of writing *the* and *&* stands for *and*. *Presents* is an old way of referring to a written document. In addition, spelling in the 1600s was much different than it is today. Here are some key parts of the Mayflower Compact, first as actually written, and then in a modern English translation:

M A Y F L O W E R   C O M P A C T

We whose names are underwritten . . . doe by these
presents solemnly & mutualy in ye presence of God, and
one of another, covenant and combine ourselves togeather into a civill body politick; for
our better ordering, & preservation & furtherance . . . and by vertue
hereof to enacte, constitute, and frame such just & equall
Lawes, ordinances, Acts, constitutions, & offices, from
time to time, as shall be thought most meete & convenient for ye generall good of ye
colonie: unto which
we promise all due submission and obedience. In witnes
whereof we have hereunder subscribed our names at
Cap-Codd ye-11-of November, in ye year . . . 1620.

MAYFLOWER COMPACT (freely modernized)

We whose names are signed below . . . do by this document solemnly, mutually, and in the presence of God and of each other, promise to join together as a single unified colony, for the good of all . . . and to make such just and equal laws and governmental frameworks, as shall be thought proper for the general good of the colony, to which we promise our loyalty. As our pledge we have signed our names at Cape Cod on November 11 in the Year . . . 1620.

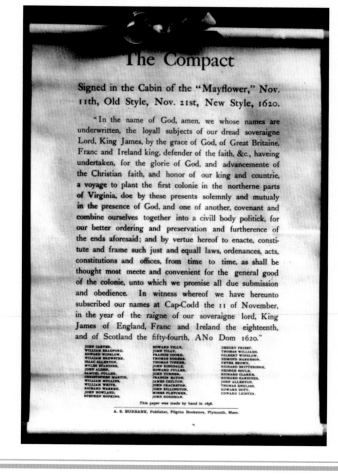

The Mayflower Compact

A page from the log of the *Mayflower* records events of its trip to the New World.

On November 11, 1620, while anchored in Provincetown Harbor, the Pilgrims listened as the **compact** was read aloud. The reading took about a minute and a half. In those days women did not take part in government. But most of the men—forty-one of them—signed the Mayflower Compact.

The document was the first agreement for self-government to take effect in what became the United States. The promise of "just & equall Lawes" for everyone satisfied the non-Separatists. They decided to remain with the rest of the group.

The landing of John Alden, Mary Chilton, and the other Pilgrims at Plymouth Rock in 1620.

CHAPTER FOUR

The Compact Helps Plymouth Survive and Grow

The Pilgrims' struggle to build a home in the New World became a famous part of American lore. In December of 1620 they settled at a spot on the Massachusetts coast. According to tradition, some of them stepped ashore over a boulder that became known as Plymouth Rock.

The Pilgrims chopped down trees and began building Plymouth, the first English town in what is now Massachusetts. About half of them died of hunger and disease during the first winter. But because the remaining Pilgrims worked together and were helped by American Indians in the area, the colony survived. To celebrate, the Pilgrims and their Native American friends held a thanksgiving celebration in the fall of 1621.

This woodcut shows Pilgrims going to worship at the first church in New England.

This gathering was a forerunner of our Thanksgiving Day, now celebrated each November in the United States.

Besides keeping the Pilgrims together, the Mayflower Compact helped Plymouth establish a remarkably **democratic government** for its time. Both Separatists and non-Separatists took part in it. For example, Separatist leader William Bradford governed the Plymouth Colony for many years. But non-Separatists such as Miles Standish and John Alden were also important to the colony. Standish, the colony's military leader, served as Plymouth's assistant governor. Alden, who eventually became a Separatist, was at times the acting governor.

Small People

People were smaller in the Pilgrims' day than they are today. The average Englishman stood about five feet six inches tall while the average Englishwoman was barely five feet in height. It was said (perhaps inaccurately) that Captain Miles Standish was only five feet two. The Native Americans called the red-haired soldier "Captain shrimp," but his bravery and leadership ability helped the Plymouth Colony survive its early years.

This photo shows a Pilgrim dealing out the daily five kernels of corn allowed each person when they came to America. Even so, half of the Pilgrims starved and died. Without help from the American Indians, the colonists would not have survived.

The Pilgrims and American Indians celebrated the survival of the colony with a Thanksgiving feast in the fall of 1621.

Myles Standish

Miles Standish sailed on the *Mayflower* and became a leader of the Plymouth colony.

During the 1620s, ships brought more Separatists and non-Separatists to Plymouth. They spread out from the original town and built new settlements in the Plymouth Colony. One town, Duxbury, was founded by Miles Standish and John Alden in 1632.

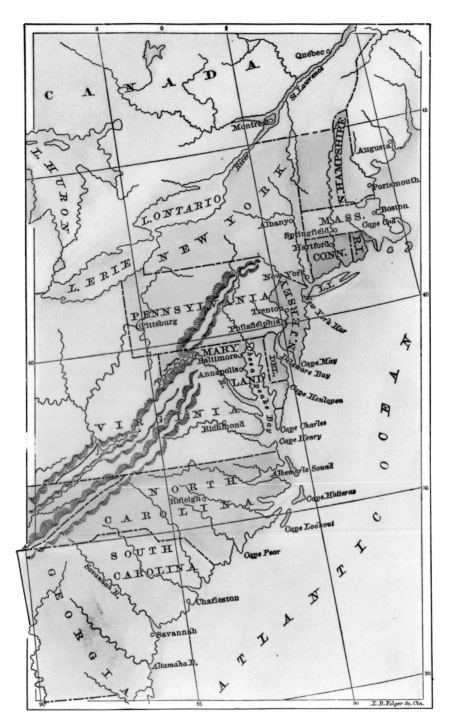

The Original Thirteen Colonies

CHAPTER FIVE

"And the Seed Is Sown"

By keeping the Pilgrims together, the Mayflower Compact helped the Plymouth Colony succeed. That was important. Partly because the Plymouth Colony lasted, England eventually established thirteen American colonies. In 1691 the Plymouth Colony was made part of the larger Massachusetts Bay Colony.

The thirteen colonies lived under English rule until 1775, when they rebelled. The next year they issued the **Declaration of Independence**. This famous document announced that the colonists were separating from England and forming a new country, the United States of America.

Many historians have claimed that the Declaration of Independence contains ideas from the Mayflower Compact. At first glance, this seems unlikely. The original copy of the Mayflower Compact was lost. For about two centuries the compact was largely forgotten. Thomas Jefferson may have known little about it when he wrote the Declaration of Independence in 1776.

Then how could the compact have influenced the declaration? It happened by **chain reaction**, historians say. As colonists built new towns in Massachusetts, they created governments like Plymouth's, even if they didn't know the exact wording of the Mayflower Compact. Massachusetts people spread to Rhode Island, New Hampshire, Connecticut, and other

A woodcut of a draft of the Declaration of Independence in Thomas Jefferson's handwriting.

colonies. They, too, brought democratic ideas to their new homes. The result was that Plymouth's example of self-government spread to many other towns and colonies. Americans also became accustomed to standing up for their rights, as the non-Separatists had done. By 1776, Americans were so used to self-government and demanding their rights that they declared their **independence**.

Crowds attend a reading of the Declaration of Independence at the Old State House in Boston, 1776.

The Colonial Settlements

The thirteen American colonies and the years in which they were first permanently settled:

Virginia	1607
Massachusetts *(then the Plymouth Colony)*	1620
New Hampshire	1623
New York	1624
Connecticut	1633
Maryland	1634
Rhode Island	1636
Delaware	1638
Pennsylvania	1643
North Carolina	1650s
New Jersey	1660
South Carolina	1670
Georgia	1733

Colonists were thrilled when independence was declared. In this woodcut, colonists tear down the king's arms on Independence Day, July 8, 1776. It became July 4 when the calendar changed.

To many people, one phrase in the Declaration of Independence best expresses what America stands for: "We hold these truths to be self-evident, that all men are created equal . . ." To a degree, these words echo the phrase "just & equall Lawes" from the Mayflower Compact. The Declaration also contains some ideas for self-government that originated in the Mayflower Compact. So, by a long process, the compact helped lead to the establishment of a new country. That is why the document created on the *Mayflower* nearly four hundred years ago has been called the seed from which America grew.

Glossary

abandon—Leave behind.

century—A period of one hundred years.

chain reaction—One action that triggers others.

colony—A settlement built by a country beyond its borders.

compact—An agreement.

Declaration of Independence—The document, issued in 1776, stating that the thirteen British colonies in America had become the United States of America.

democratic government—A government in which there is strong participation by the people.

document—An official paper.

independence—Freedom or self-government.

Mayflower Compact—Created by the Pilgrims aboard the *Mayflower* in November 1620, this was the first agreement for self-government instituted in what is now the United States.

mutiny—A revolt.

non-Separatists—A name for the Pilgrims who were not Separatists.

peninsula—Land surrounded by water on three sides.

permanent—Lasting.

pilgrims—People who travel to distant lands, often for religious reasons.

Pilgrims—With a capital P, this refers to the people, both Separatists and non-Separatists, who founded Plymouth, Massachusetts, in 1620.

rituals—Ways of doing things in the same way each time, usually connected to religion.

Separatists—People who broke away from the Church of England.

Timeline

1607—Virginia Colony, England's first permanent American colony, is begun; in this year, Separatists in Scrooby, England, are persecuted

1608—Most of the Scrooby Separatists flee to the Netherlands

1609—By now the Scrooby Separatists have settled in the city of Leiden in the Netherlands

1620—**September 6:** Pilgrims sail from England on the *Mayflower*
November 9: Pilgrims sight land
November 11: Mayflower Compact signed
December 16: Pilgrims anchor at Plymouth

1621—Pilgrims and Indians hold thanksgiving celebration that is a forerunner of our modern Thanksgiving Day

1607　　**1620**　　*1621*

1691—Plymouth
Colony is made part
of Massachusetts

1775—Thirteen colonies
rebel against English rule

1776—Americans issue Declaration of
Independence, which was partly inspired
by the Mayflower Compact

1970—Mayflower
Compact's three hundred
and fiftieth anniversary

2020—Mayflower Compact's
four hundredth anniversary

1691   *1775*   *1970*   *2020*

Further Information

F O R   F U R T H E R   R E A D I N G

Arenstam, Peter, John Kemp, and Catherine O'Neill Grace. *Mayflower 1620: A New Look at a Pilgrim Voyage.* Washington, DC: National Geographic, 2003.

Davis, Kenneth C. *Don't Know Much About the Pilgrims.* New York: HarperCollins, 2002.

Donovan, Frank R. *The Mayflower Compact.* New York: Grosset & Dunlap, 1968.

Richards, Norman. *The Story of the Mayflower Compact*. Chicago: Childrens Press, 1967.

Riehecky, Janet. *The Plymouth Colony*. Milwaukee: World Almanac, 2002.

Walsh, John E. *The Mayflower Compact, November 11, 1620: The First Democratic Document in America*. New York: Franklin Watts, 1971.

Whitehurst, Susan. *Plymouth: Surviving the First Winter*. New York: Rosen, 2002.

For information on the Mayflower Compact from the Pilgrim Hall Museum
http://www.pilgrimhall.org/compcon.htm

For information on the Mayflower Compact
http://home.nc.rr.com/ncmayflower/MayflowerCompact.htm

For information on Pilgrim children aboard the Mayflower
http://home.nc.rr.com/ncmayflower/Children.htm

For information on the Pilgrims
http://www.mayflower.org/pilgrim.htm

For information and pictures of the re-created Pilgrims' Plymouth settlement
http://pilgrims.net/plimothplantation/vtour/index.htm

Bibliography

Bradford, William. *Of Plymouth Plantation: 1620–1647*. New York: Knopf (1963 edition of Bradford's manuscript from the 1600s).

Cowie, Leonard W. *The Pilgrim Fathers*. London: Wayland, 1970.

Dillon, Francis. *The Pilgrims*. Garden City, NY: Doubleday, 1975.

Gill, Crispin. *Mayflower Remembered: A History of the Plymouth Pilgrims*. Newton Abbot, England: David & Charles, 1970.

Haxtun, Annie Arnoux. *Signers of the Mayflower Compact* (3 parts in 1 volume). New York: Reprinted from the *Mail and Express*, 1896–1899.

Morison, Samuel Eliot. *The Story of the "Old Colony" of New Plymouth*. New York: Knopf, 1956.

Index

Page numbers in **boldface** are illustrations.

About the Author

Dennis Fradin is the author of 150 books, some of them written with his wife Judith Bloom Fradin. Their recent book for Clarion, *The Power of One: Daisy Bates and the Little Rock Nine*, was named a Golden Kite Honor Book. Another of Dennis's recent books is *Let It Begin Here! Lexington & Concord: First Battles of the American Revolution*, published by Walker. The Fradins are currently writing a biography of social worker and anti-war activist Jane Addams for Clarion and a nonfiction book about a slave escape for National Geographic Children's Books. Turning Points in U.S. History is Dennis Fradin's first series for Marshall Cavendish Benchmark. The Fradins have three grown children and three young grandchildren.